UL   2009

ADAPTED FOR SUCCESS

EAGLES
AND OTHER BIRDS

Andrew Solway

Heinemann Library
Chicago, Illinois

Photo research by Mica Brancic and Susi Paz
Designed by Richard Parker
Printed and bound in China by WKT Company Ltd

11 10 09 08 07
10 9 8 7 6 5 4 3 2 1

Library of Congress Cataloging-in-Publication Data
Solway, Andrew.
  Eagles and other birds / Andrew Solway.
     p. cm. -- (Adapted for success)
  Includes bibliographical references and index.
  ISBN-13: 978-1-4034-8222-8 (library binding (hardcover))
  ISBN-10: 1-4034-8222-5
  ISBN-13: 978-1-4034-8229-7 (pbk.)
  ISBN-10: 1-4034-8229-2
  1. Eagles--Juvenile literature. 2. Birds--Juvenile literature. I. Title. II. Series: Solway, Andrew. Adapted for success.
  QL696.F32S65 2006
  598.9'42--dc22

                         2006014291

Acknowledgments
The author and publisher are grateful to the following for permission to reproduce copyright material:
Alamy pp. 24 (Blickwinkel), 10 (Bruce Coleman Inc.), 22 (Westend61); Corbis pp. 4, 20, 32, 38, 40, 41, pp. 29 (Tim Zurowski), 28 (W. Perry Conway); FLPA p. 33 (Minden); Getty Images pp. 15 (Aurora), 25 (Dorling Kindersley), 6, 31 (National Geographic), 5, 12 (PhotoDisc), 7, 16 (Taxi), 14 (The Image Bank); LeeAbley.com p. 30; NHPA pp. 23 (Alan Williams), 27 (James Warwick), 26 (Mike Lane), 32 (Roger Tidman); Oxford Scientific Films pp. 11, 39 (Mark Hamblin), 35 (Robin Bush), 37 (Terry Heathcote); PhotoDisc p. 18 (Harcourt); Science Photo Library pp. 21 (E. R. Degginger), 34 (Jim Zipp), 19 (John Beatty).

Cover photograph of a bald eagle with ruffled feathers reproduced with permission of Acclaim Images (Ardea/ Jim Zipp).

The publishers would like to thank Ann Fullick for her assistance in the preparation of this book.

Every effort has been made to contact copyright holders of any material reproduced in this book. Any omissions will be rectified in subsequent printings if notice is given to the publisher.

Contents

Some words are shown in bold, **like this**. You can find out what they mean by looking in the glossary.

An Introduction to Birds

A golden eagle soars into the sky, its broad wings spread. It circles effortlessly upward until it is just a dot. Yet, even from that height, the eagle can spot a rabbit leaving its burrow.

Eagles are well adapted for soaring and for hunting. An **adaptation** is a change that helps a living thing survive in its **habitat**.

Emperor penguins are the only vertebrates that spend winter on land in the Antarctic.

Success story

Birds are a very successful group of animals, but what does it mean to be successful? One measure of success is the number of **species** in a group. Birds are the biggest group of **vertebrates**, other than fish, so by this measure they are definitely successful.

The **range** of a group (the places where it lives) is another measure of success. Birds are also successful by this measure. Birds are found in just about every environment on Earth. There are penguins in the Antarctic and sand grouse in the hottest deserts. Bar-headed geese fly high over the highest mountains, while emperor penguins dive deep beneath the ocean surface. No other vertebrate has such a wide range.

WHAT IS A BIRD?

Birds are vertebrates, as are amphibians, mammals, reptiles, and fish. Unlike all other vertebrates, however, birds have feathers. Birds also have wings, even if they cannot fly.

Like mammals, birds are **warm-blooded**, which means that they can keep their bodies warm even if their surroundings are cold. They **reproduce** by laying eggs with a hard shell, which hatch into baby birds.

Secrets of success

What are the secrets of birds' success? The two most important factors are probably feathers and flight. Birds have feathers because they are **warm-blooded**. The first birds had scales like reptiles, but they adapted into feathers. Feathers provided better insulation, keeping heat in and cold out. The feathers help keep a bird's body temperature constant, whatever the temperature of the air may be. This is what it means to be warm-blooded. Because of their insulation, birds can live in both very hot and very cold places.

Feathers also are an important part of a bird's wings, which they use for flying. Being able to fly allows birds to eat foods that other animals cannot eat, such as flying insects. They also are able to live or nest in places other animals cannot reach, such as cliff ledges. Flying has allowed birds to spread far quickly, even over oceans and mountain ranges.

Birds of prey

There are approximately 515 different birds of **prey**—birds that hunt and kill animals for food. This includes around 309 species that hunt by day, and around 206 owls, which hunt mostly at night. Birds of prey make up just a small part of the 9,845 known species of birds.

Eagles are part of the largest group of birds of prey, known as **accipiters** (hawks). There are 59 species of eagle, including booted eagles, fish eagles, and snake eagles, but several other large accipiters also are called eagles. The group also includes hawks, buzzards, and some vultures.

Eagles, vultures, and other large birds of prey are experts at soaring flight. They use warm, rising currents of air to carry them up to great heights.

Adaptation and Natural Selection

How have birds adapted to fit into so many different environments? **Evolution** is the process by which life on Earth has developed and changed. Life first appeared on Earth 3.5 billion years ago. Since then, living things have evolved from simple single **cells** to the estimated 10 million or more different species on Earth today.

Vultures are hawks, but they are adpated for feeding on dead **carcasses** rather than catching live prey.

Useful changes

Adaptation is an important part of evolution. Adaptations are ways in which a living thing changes to fit into a particular environment and way of life. For instance, a penguin's thick layer of fat is an adaptation to help it keep warm even in the water, and an eagle's curved, pointed beak is adapted for digging into flesh and tearing off pieces of meat.

Birds and other living things do not choose their adaptations. Two mechanisms make adaptations happen. They are **variation** and **natural selection**.

Variation

Not all individuals of the same species are exactly the same. You can see this yourself if you look around your class at school. Some people are taller than others. Some people have light hair, while others have dark hair. Some people are musical, and some are good at sports. These differences among individuals of a species are known as variations.

Natural selection

Variation among individuals is what makes it possible for a species to change and adapt. The driving force that makes this happen is natural selection.

In any environment, there are only a limited number of ways living things can get food. Different species compete with each other for food, for space, and for **mates**. The animals that are most successful at getting food and space are able to grow and reproduce. They pass on their useful characteristics to their **offspring**.

If there are changes in the environment where a species lives, natural selection will help the species adapt. For example, birds of a widespread species, such as the golden eagle, are larger in cold areas than in warm ones. This is because a larger animal loses heat more slowly than a small one, so it is easier for a large animal to keep warm in cold weather.

ALL IN THE GENES

Living things pass on characteristics to their offspring through their **genes**. A living thing's genetic material is a kind of instruction book for that individual.

Most animals and plants produce offspring by sexual reproduction. Males and females each produce special cells, known as **gametes**, which have only half the normal genetic material. Each parent provides half the genetic information for the offspring.

When gannets gather together to breed, they use every available inch of space for nesting sites.

Adapted to Fly

Although there are many different kinds of birds, they have some basic things in common. Most of these similarities are adaptations for flight.

Three main adaptations

Birds are adapted for flight in these three main ways:

- Birds are lighter than land mammals, so they need less energy for flying.
- Birds are more compact than land mammals. Most of their weight is concentrated close to the center of the body. This makes them more stable and maneuverable (able to twist and turn) in flight.
- A bird's lungs are adapted to keep the flight muscles supplied with plenty of oxygen while the bird is flying.

One-way breathing

Birds have very different lungs from other land mammals. The lungs themselves are small and stiff. They do not expand and contract as human lungs do. Instead, a bird's lungs have a set of balloon-like air sacs that supply air to the lungs. Birds have a separate entry and exit to their lungs. The air they breathe goes into one set of air sacs and then into the lungs. Then it moves into some different air sacs before it is breathed out altogether. The advantage of this system is that air always moves through the lungs in the same direction, and the air in the lungs is fresh and full of oxygen. In human lungs, on the other hand, there is always some stale air remaining.

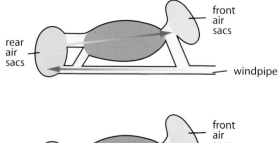

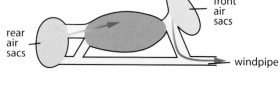

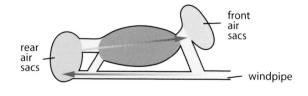

It takes four breaths (two in, two out) for a bird to go through its complete breathing cycle.

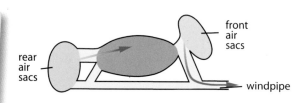

NOT JUST FOR FLYING

A bird's feathers do many different jobs. They insulate a bird's body, keeping it warm in cold weather and cool in hot weather. The long, stiff wing feathers increase the area of the wings and give them the right shape for flight. The outer feathers on the body **streamline** the bird's shape, so that it slips easily through the air. The colors and patterns on the feathers sometimes help **camouflage** the bird, or they may be bright colors that are important for courtship and mating.

Light and stiff

The biggest differences between birds and other vertebrates are in their skeletons. The individual bones of a bird's skeleton are very light because they are full of large air spaces. The backbone is short and the individual vertebrae (bones of the back) are fused (joined). This makes the body stiffer and more compact (packed tightly). The tail bones also are small and fused together.

A bird's skull is much lighter than that of other animals. Birds have large eyes, so the eye sockets are huge. Birds do not have the heavy lower jaw and teeth of other vertebrates. Instead, they have a much lighter **bill**.

The bones of a bird's front limbs are greatly changed to work as wings. Finally, the sternum (breastbone) is extended down into a large flat area called the keel. This is where the flight muscles attach.

Big muscles

A bird's main muscles are the large pectoral (chest) muscles that power flight. The main power comes on the downstroke, so the muscles that pull the wings down are much bigger than those that lift them up again. Eagles and most other birds of prey also have strong muscles for gripping prey with their **talons**.

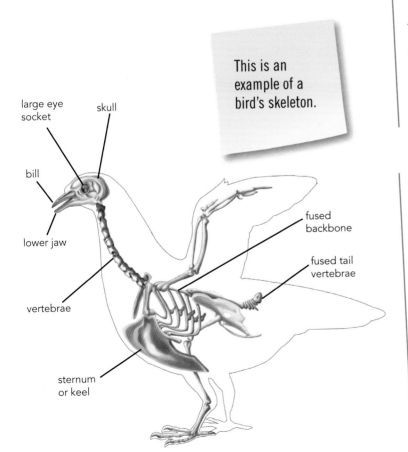

This is an example of a bird's skeleton.

large eye socket

skull

bill

lower jaw

vertebrae

sternum or keel

fused backbone

fused tail vertebrae

9

Eagle Habitats

Different eagle species live in a range of different habitats. Each species has some adaptations that suit its particular habitat.

Definite preferences

Most eagle species are found in particular habitats. Harpy eagles live in dense South American rainforests, while steppe eagles live on the open Russian steppes (grassy plains). In Africa, bateleur eagles live mostly on **savannah** grasslands and other areas of open country, while fish eagles live alongside rivers or by the sea. Golden eagles are found in many places around the world, but they usually live in mountain or upland areas at high altitude.

Habitat adaptations

All eagles have a similar body plan because they all live and feed in similar ways. However, different species have adaptations to their particular habitat. For instance, eagles that live in forests have shorter wings and longer tails than other eagles. Shorter wings take up less space, and a long tail makes it easier to twist and turn in flight. Both of these adaptations make it easier for forest eagles to chase their prey through the dense space of a forest.

Eagles that live in open country, such as bateleur and steppe eagles, have longer, broader wings and short, wide tails. These adaptations are much better for soaring flight. Soaring eagles can search large areas of land for prey. This is very important in regions where prey is scarce. Bateleur eagles may spend most of the day in the air, flying up to 200 miles (320 kilometers) in search of prey.

Like other forest eagles, harpy eagles have relatively short wings adapted for chasing prey in the forest.

Non-specialists

Eagles are mostly **specialists** that live in particular habitats, but other hawks can live in a much wider range of environments. For example, Eurasian kestrels, a species of kestrel found in Europe and Asia, live in all kinds of habitats, from hot deserts to cold Arctic lands. They also have adapted to living in towns and cities. Common buzzards are another **generalist** species. Many buzzards have adapted to human environments by using telephone poles as perching posts from which to watch for prey.

The white-tailed eagle often lives along coasts in northern Europe and Asia. Its strongly curved talons and rough feet are adapted for gripping slippery fish.

RIDING THE AIR CURRENTS

Eagles are the masters of soaring flight. This uses much less energy than flapping flight because the air does a lot of the work. To soar, eagles need to find small patches of warm, rising air, known as **thermals**. The eagles can ride these thermals to a great height using their broad wings to get plenty of lift. They glide around and around in tight spirals in order to keep moving and remain in the thermal.

At the top of the thermal, the eagle launches itself into a long, shallow glide. While gliding, eagles slowly lose height until they find a new thermal. Eagles can travel long distances and even **migrate** this way. They have difficulty flying over the sea, however, as there are no thermals over water.

Birds in Every Habitat

Birds have adapted to fit into a large number of different habitats. Although there are many birds in colder regions, the largest number of species live in the tropics, which are warm areas close to the Equator. The rainforests of South America, Africa, and Southeast Asia are especially rich in birds.

Macaws, like this one, and other types of parrot have two forward-pointing toes and two pointing backward.

Different feet

A bird's feet say a lot about where it lives, and sometimes about how it feeds. Birds that live in forests have feet that are adapted to perching on trees. Most have three toes pointing forward and one toe pointing backward. This allows them to grip branches between their toes. Swifts, on the other hand, have short legs and tiny, weak feet. They can perch on the edge of a nest, but they cannot walk on the ground. This is because swifts spend most of their lives in the air.

Waterbirds—such as ducks, geese, and gulls—do not have this backward-pointing toe. They have webbed feet that they use as paddles, with all four toes pointing forward.

The feet of eagles and their relatives are adapted to the food they eat. An eagle's legs and feet are short and strong, while their talons are long and curved. They have a strong grip for catching and holding large prey such as rabbits. Sparrow hawks have long legs and toes, and thin, needle-sharp talons for catching birds in flight. Ospreys have very curved claws and rough scales on their toes to hold slippery fish, which are their main prey.

Wing shape

Another important adaptation to different habitats is wing shape. Most forest birds have short wings for quick turns as they fly between trees (as shown in the example of the harpy eagle on page 10). Many seabirds have long, narrow wings, like a glider. This is because they spend a lot of their time in flight, so they glide whenever possible to save energy.

Penguins have short, strong wings that they use for swimming. They can glide in the water, but not in the air. A few birds, such as puffins and auks, can glide underwater and also through the air.

The fastest fliers, such as swifts and peregrine falcons, have narrow, swept-back wings. This wing shape also makes them very agile because they can change direction in an instant.

LIFE IN THE DARK

Cave swiftlets spend their whole lives in caves in Southeast Asia. To find their way around in the dark, swiftlets use an **echolocation** system similar to that of bats and dolphins. A swiftlet sends out a string of high-pitched clicks as it flies. The sounds bounce off the objects around the swiftlet, and it hears the echoes as they return. From the patterns of these returning echoes, the swiftlet can build up a mental picture of its surroundings.

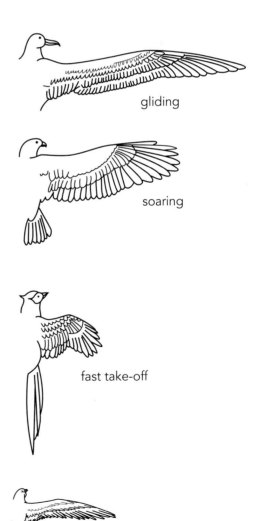

gliding

soaring

fast take-off

high speed

The shape of a bird's wing is adapted to its lifestyle and where it lives.

Powerful Predators

Eagles have many adaptations related to getting food. They are a large **predator** adapted to catch large prey such as other birds, rabbits, and even monkeys.

Hunting weapons

Like most birds of prey, eagles hunt with their feet. Their main weapons are their talons—the large, curved claws on their very strong feet. Eagles combine their talons with a high-speed attack. A golden eagle swoops in low behind its prey, rises quickly at the last moment, then drops at quick speed to strike the animal with great force.

An eagle's deep, hooked beak looks like a powerful weapon, but in fact eagles do not use their beaks to attack prey. The beak is adapted for ripping flesh from a carcass.

Fed up

When an eagle makes a large kill, it will eat as much as it can in one meal. After this it will not need to hunt for several days. Eating huge meals in this way is an adaptation found in most predators. If a predator makes the most of the prey it catches, it is more likely to survive if there is a shortage of prey for some reason.

SNAKE EAGLES

The bateleur eagle is one of a group of smaller eagles called snake eagles. These eagles eat mainly snakes, reptiles, and **carrion**. Snake eagles have long legs covered in thick scales that protect them from snakebites. They also usually have a crest on their head. When it finds a snake, a snake eagle raises its crest and spreads its wings to distract the snake from more vulnerable parts of its body, such as the breast. The eagle then attacks with its feet.

Sharp senses

All predators need sharp senses in order to find and track their prey. Eagles rely mainly on their eyesight to find food. An eagle soaring at 1,640 feet (500 meters) can see over a large area and can spot a rabbit moving from 1 mile (1.6 kilometers) away.

An eagle's vision is so good because its eyes are large and gather huge amounts of light. Also, the retina (the light-sensitive part at the back of the eye) is tightly packed with light-sensitive cells. Like other birds, eagles can see in color. Most mammals see in black and white. Only humans and some other **primates** see in color. Even human color vision, however, is not as good as an eagle's eyesight. This is because eagles and other birds can see ultraviolet light (a kind of invisible light beyond the violet end of the spectrum) in addition to the colors that humans can see.

This is a scorpion seen under ultraviolet light. Could this be what an eagle sees as it searches for prey?

Feeding Adaptations

Not all birds are predators like eagles. Some birds are plant-eaters, while others feed entirely on insects. Some birds are **omnivores**. They feed on insects when they are a plentiful food source, and eat seeds and other plant foods when insects are scarce.

Plant-eaters

Many birds eat mainly plants. Most ducks, geese, and swans feed on grass and other plants on land, or on waterweed and other plants in the water. Sparrows and finches are among some of the large number of bird species that eat mainly seeds. In the tropics, some birds live entirely on fruit.

A **diet** of plant food is often not very nutritious. Seeds do not provide enough protein, while leafy plant foods contain large amounts of a substance called cellulose, which birds cannot digest. Birds adapt in different ways to this poor diet. Seed-eaters occasionally eat insects to increase the amount of protein they eat. Ducks, geese, and other birds that eat leaves have to feed for most of each day in order to get enough nutrition from their food.

Demoiselle cranes migrate long distances each year. They spend winter in northern Africa and India, then fly to Central Asia in the summer to breed.

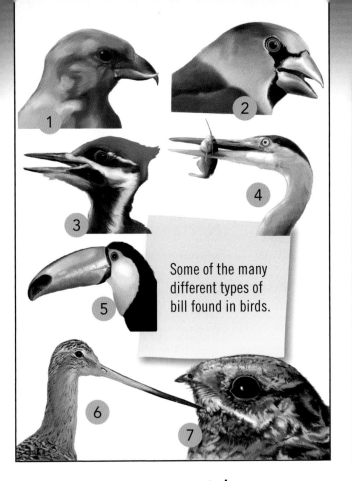

Some of the many different types of bill found in birds.

Some birds have to travel to find food at certain times of the year. Many insect-eaters living in temperate (mild) climates migrate to warmer areas in autumn when the insect supply runs out. They return in the spring to mate and nest.

Arctic terns make the longest migrations of all. They breed in the Arctic, then travel to the Antarctic to avoid the Arctic summer. This is a round trip of about 22,400 miles (36,000 kilometers) each year.

The right bill for the job

One important adaptation to a particular way of feeding is a bird's bill (beak).

- Insect-eaters tend to have narrow bills that can snap up fast-moving insects very quickly. Flying insect-eaters (7) can open their mouths very wide, which gives them a better chance of catching insects.

- Seed-eaters have deeper, stronger bills for breaking seeds. The hawfinch (2) has a very strong beak that can crack open olive stones, and a toucan's huge beak (5) can crack open brazil nuts. The ends of a crossbill's beak (1) cross over each other, which allows it to pull the scales off pine cones and get at the seeds underneath.

- Many wading birds have long bills (6) that they use to probe in the mud for worms and other creatures. Ducks have broad bills so that they can shovel up big mouthfuls of water and filter out the food particles.

Because birds feed in different ways, many different species can survive in the same area.

Feeding other ways

Insect-eating birds feed in many different ways. Swifts, swallows, and martins hunt flying insects on the wing. Bee-eaters and flycatchers dart out from a perch to catch flying insects. Birds such as woodpeckers (3) and treecreepers dig out insects from under the bark of trees. Kiwis probe the ground sniffing for insects. They are one of the few birds that uses smell to find its prey.

Some birds catch animals other than insects. Many seabirds, waterbirds, and some birds of prey feed on fish (4). Other birds of prey hunt birds, reptiles, or mammals.

Unusual Feeders

In most habitats the competition for plentiful foods, such as insects or berries, can be extremely fierce. Some birds avoid this competition altogether by adapting to make use of unusual foods. Other birds have found unique ways to feed.

Some flowers rely on hummingbirds to pollinate them (to carry pollen from one flower to another). These plants have long tubular flowers, and only a hummingbird's long beak can reach the nectar.

Nectar-drinkers

Hummingbirds are specialists in drinking **nectar** from flowers. Most hummingbirds have long beaks to reach deep into the flower they are visiting. They also have a long tongue, which in some hummingbirds is rolled into two tubes, like a double drinking straw, for sucking up the nectar.

Hummingbirds have adapted to feeding on nectar by evolving amazing powers of flight. To feed, hummingbirds hover in front of each flower they visit, and beat their wings around 60 times per second to hold themselves still. Nectar is a high-energy food source, which is good because hovering uses large amounts of energy. An active hummingbird uses more energy for its weight than any other vertebrate.

CROCODILE BIRDS

A few birds rely on other animals for food. Black-backed coursers are commonly called crocodile birds because they get their food from crocodiles. They hop over the crocodile's body, picking out **parasites** from its hide and eating them. They may even climb inside the crocodile's mouth to look for tasty treats!

Food strainers

Flamingos feed in salt lakes where the water is so full of natural chemicals that hardly anything can live there. The flamingos eat **algae** and other small creatures that they find on the bottom of the lake.

Flamingos have a unique bill that acts like a very fine filter. The flamingo bends down and puts its beak in the water, then uses its tongue to suck water into the bill and push it out again up to twenty times every second. The bill allows water to flow out, but stops food items from escaping.

Pirates of the open seas

Some seabirds get food by piracy. Frigate birds, skuas, and jaegers are well-known pirates. They attack seabirds, such as gannets and terns, in the air, and force their victims to drop or **regurgitate** food that they have caught.

No pirate bird species relies entirely on piracy for its food. However, piracy is an adaptation that can help a species survive. For example, frigate birds are large sea predators that feed on flying fish, squid, and other animals that they snatch from the surface of the water. (Frigate birds cannot dive beneath the surface because their feathers are not waterproof.) An adult frigate bird is very good at snatching up prey in this way, but it may take younger frigate birds several years to master this technique. To supplement their diet, the younger birds turn to piracy and steal from diving birds. In this way, they are able to enjoy food from below the surface without diving for it themselves.

A greater flamingo feeds in a lagoon. Flamingos feed in shallow water, usually where the lake bed is muddy.

19

Keeping a Low Profile

Many birds use camouflage to hide themselves. Often this is an adaptation of prey animals to hide from predators. Birds of prey also use camouflage to help them sneak up on prey. Many eagles and other hawks are brownish or grayish, sometimes with barred patterns on their chest. These colors help them blend in with their environment.

Eagles do not dive on their prey from a great height as peregrine falcons do. A fast, steep dive is good for catching flying prey, but a low approach is better for prey on the ground or in the water.

Disguising an attack

Eagles use other methods to help them sneak up on prey. An eagle soaring high in the sky is not visible to prey animals, yet its excellent eyesight allows it to scan a wide area for possible victims. Once it has seen its prey, the eagle approaches on a low, fast, silent glide. Then it rises at the last moment before dropping onto its victim.

Some smaller hawks use the landscape to stay hidden from their prey. Sparrow hawks and goshawks often hunt in woodlands. They are fast, agile flyers that prey on other birds. Sparrow hawks also hunt in more open areas by flying fast and low, and flipping over hedges and around trees or bushes in the hope of surprising a group of birds on the other side. By using natural features in this way, sparrow hawks can get close to their prey without being discovered.

Camouflaged hunters

Day-hunting birds of prey have some camouflage, but owls are much better camouflaged. Most owls are nocturnal. This means they hunt at night. When they are resting during the day, owls need to hide themselves to avoid predators, so many of them are camouflaged.

Camouflage also disguises owls from flocks of small birds, which sometimes **mob** owls during the day. When small birds mob a larger bird, a group of them dive at it, calling loudly. This warns other birds in the area that an enemy is nearby. It may also drive the predator out of the area.

Snowy owls live in and around the Arctic where they nest on the ground. Their white **plumage** provides excellent camouflage when they are sitting on the nest.

EGGS OR PEBBLES?

Eagles usually build large nests in trees or on cliffs. Here the eggs are safe from many predators, but good climbers such as tree snakes and martens can often reach them. The eggs are, therefore, camouflaged for extra protection.

Other birds, such as ringed plovers, which are also camouflaged, lay their eggs on pebble beaches in cold parts of the world. Each egg is colored and patterned to look like a pebble. However, Arctic foxes and other predators still find many of the eggs.

The white plumage of snowy owls makes them difficult to see on snowy ground.

Hiding from Enemies

Eagles are often **top predators** in their habitat, which means they have few natural enemies. Other birds have many more predators than eagles, and camouflage is one way that they avoid being eaten.

Ringed plover chicks are defended by their parents until they **fledge** (learn to fly) at 21 to 42 days old.

Ground cover

Camouflage is especially important for ground birds at nesting time. Ground-nesting birds, such as ringed plovers, have well-camouflaged eggs (see page 21). The young chicks are also extremely well camouflaged when they hatch. Their nest is a shallow hole in the ground, but if they stay still, the chicks are almost impossible to see.

Many ground-living birds have mottled (blotchy) or barred plumage that gives good camouflage. Nightjars have barred patterns that blend in with the forest where they live. Snipes are colored and patterned to be invisible among reeds, while sand grouse are almost impossible to see when they are nesting on sandy ground in the desert.

Colorful camouflage

Parrots are well known for having brightly colored plumage. Some species are mainly green and yellow, but many species have bright reds, oranges, and blues in their plumage. These bright colors are good camouflage in the tropical rainforests where most parrots live. Their bright colors look like flowers among the leaves, or patches of bright sunlight.

The right position

For camouflage to work, a bird must stay completely still or it will be seen. The position the bird freezes in is also important. Many birds crouch down when they sense danger. Crouching makes a bird smaller and reduces its shadow.

Bitterns do not crouch to hide themselves. Bitterns live among tall reeds where a crouched shape would show up among the reed stalks. Instead, bitterns stick their beak straight up into the air and make themselves as long and thin as possible. This position, combined with their streaky brown plumage, gives them great camouflage.

This bittern is in its camouflage pose. Bitterns are relatives of herons. There are thirteen different species of bittern around the world.

CHANGING COLOR

In cold northern parts of the world, the ground can be covered in snow for six months of the year. Ptarmigans, a kind of grouse, have brownish-gray plumage during the summer, but in winter this plumage would stand out against the snow. So they have evolved an adaptation to keep them camouflaged through the winter. When winter snows come, ptarmigans **molt**. They lose their gray-brown feathers and grow a new white plumage.

Defense

Eagles are top predators, so it may seem that they should not need to defend themselves against threats. Large eagle adults do not have any real predators other than humans (see pages 38–39). Yet eagles can be at risk when they are young. They also often have to defend themselves from other eagles of the same species.

Threat displays

An eagle's adaptations for defense are the same as those it uses for attacking its prey—its talons and beak, for warding off attack, and its wings, to escape from danger. When eagles are threatened, they usually respond with a threat display of their own. This can involve special threat calls, raising the feathers on the head and neck, stretching the head forward, and opening the wings.

Threat displays are most often used between eagles of the same species, particularly during the breeding season. Any other eagle coming into the **territory** is threatened. Usually this is enough to make the stranger leave. Sometimes, however, the eagles may fight, locking talons in an aerial (sky) battle. One eagle will usually break away before there is any serious injury.

Eagles are also aggressive to other animals—even humans—when they are nesting, especially when they have young chicks. Anyone accidentally getting too close to an eagle's nest at such a time is likely to be attacked.

A martial eagle confronts a warthog. The eagle opens its wings to make itself look more threatening.

Eagle chicks learn defensive behaviour from a very early age. They lie low in the nest and freeze if a predator is nearby. As a last resort the chicks lie on their backs and strike at an attacker with their talons.

Not safe on the ground

An eagle can be at risk when it is on the ground. This is because eagles are heavy birds. Although they can soar, dive, and swoop in the air, they are poor fliers when it comes to flapping flight. A large eagle cannot get off the ground quickly, especially if it has eaten. For this reason, eagles will often carry prey away to a perch where they can eat more safely.

RISKY TIME

Eagles are most at risk from predators when they are chicks. To keep their chicks safe, parents often camouflage the nest with plant material. While the chicks are young, female eagles spend most of their time at the nest or close by, ready to scare off any danger.

Once they begin to move around, eagle chicks perch near the nest rather than stay in it. This may be because they are less visible to predators when perching.

Flocking Together

Other birds have many more enemies than eagles. Most species are hunted by snakes, many kinds of mammal, and birds of prey. Different birds have different defenses against predators. One of the most common defenses is to gather together in flocks.

A mixed flock of cranes, whooper swans, gulls, and other birds feed together at Lake Hornborg in Sweden.

Safety in numbers

Some birds feed together in flocks. Others feed alone during the day, then gather together at night to rest in **roosts**. In many cities in Europe and the United States, starlings gather together in the evenings in large flocks, sometimes as many as thousands of birds. They fly around the sky together for a while before heading off to a roost.

Feeding or roosting in flocks has survival advantages, particularly for smaller birds. One bird by itself cannot have eyes and ears everywhere at once. In a large flock, however, there are many eyes and ears to watch for enemies.

If a bird spots a predator, it gives an alarm call, and the whole flock then rises into the air as one compact group. The flock swerves and turns, but the birds always stay close together.

Birds of prey will not dive at a tight flock of birds. This is partly because it is hard to pick out an individual bird as a target. Another reason is that the bird of prey might crash into birds in the flock and be injured. Instead, a bird of prey will wait around the edges of a flock and watch for slower birds. Any bird that is left behind is much more likely to be attacked.

Forest flocks

In many woodlands and forests, especially in tropical areas, birds sometimes feed together in mixed flocks. The birds in the flock eat a range of foods at different levels in the forest. Scientists think that this kind of group feeding improves the chances for individual birds to find food. There is also the benefit of being safer from predators in a flock. One species of bird usually keeps the mixed flock together with regular calls.

THE BIGGEST FLOCKS

The red-billed quelea is probably the most numerous bird in the world. Queleas are seed-eaters that live in Africa. Flocks of red-billed queleas can contain millions of birds. They are such a pest to farmers that they are nicknamed locust birds.

Queleas are a kind of weaver bird (see page 37). They nest together in large colonies that can cover up to 250 acres (100 hectares), which is the area of a medium-sized farm.

Staying together

Scientists wondered for many years how flocks of birds, such as these red-billed queleas, can stay together in such tight groups when they are constantly changing direction. Studies have shown that flocks do not have a leader telling them what to do. Instead, if a bird changes direction in a way that takes them into the flock, other birds around will follow and also turn. A wave of turning spreads out from one bird, and soon the whole flock is heading in a new direction.

Scaring Off the Enemy

Camouflage and flocking are two of the most important defenses that birds use against their enemies. However, many birds have also evolved other ways to avoid or escape predators.

Young long-eared owls fluff up their feathers and fan out their wings in an impressive threat display.

Sounding an alarm

Sound is an important way to communicate for most birds. Birds use calls for various purposes, and one important purpose is to sound the alarm. An alarm call from one bird warns all other birds in the area that there is an enemy nearby.

If the predator is a bird of prey, a group of small birds may mob it by calling and diving repeatedly at it. Attacking a bird of prey may seem dangerous, but with several attackers it is difficult for the predator to know which bird to chase. In any case, most birds of prey are not quick enough to catch small, agile birds without the advantages of surprise and being able to dive from a height. Often the predator will move on because, once birds know it is there, it cannot hunt them.

Wrynecks, a type of woodpecker, get their name from their threat display. When threatened, they move their heads in snake-like movements and hiss. This display is very effective against smaller predators.

Most ground-nesting birds rely on good camouflage to keep their nests safe from predators. If a predator gets too close, however, the birds will often try to distract them away from the nest. If a bird is on the nest, it will remain still until the predator gets very close. Then it flies up, calling in alarm. The sudden flurry of movement distracts the predator from the nest. Plovers, jaegers, and nightjars sometimes hop away from an enemy, pretending to be injured. They lure the predator away from the nest, then fly away when it has gone.

Nest defenses

Birds escape from many predators by simply flying away when threatened. When they are nesting, however, birds have to stay in one place for long periods of time. This places them at risk. So many kinds of birds build nests that help defend them against predators. Whistling thrushes nest very close to, or even behind, waterfalls. Orioles build nests over water or near wasps' nests. Penduline tits defend their nests in different ways. Some African species build fortress nests made almost entirely of thorn twigs. Other penduline tits hide the real nest entrance and make a false entrance that comes to a dead end.

Plovers and other ground-nesting birds pretend to be injured to lure predators away from the nest. This killdeer pretends to have a broken wing.

How Eagles Live

Eagles live and hunt alone for part of the year, but during the breeding season they pair up with another eagle to mate, lay eggs, and bring up young. Eagles that breed in colder regions migrate to warmer feeding areas for the winter.

Finding a mate

Like many birds, eagles have only one mate in a year. Some eagles take the same mate for several years and possibly for life. Each eagle pair lives in a particular area, called its territory, which it defends against strangers. Usually they use the same territory each year. The eagles hunt over a larger area, called their **home range**. The home range is too big for the eagles to defend, and it may overlap with the home ranges of other eagles.

Before mating, eagles make amazing courtship flights. The pairs chase each other, dive, soar, and circle together. Fish eagles fly high into the sky, then hold each other's talons and tumble down in whirling cartwheels.

Eagles and other hawks use all their flying skills in amazing courtship displays.

Raising young

Once eagles have chosen their partners and mated, the female lays her eggs in a nest. In eagles and other birds of prey, the female does most of the sitting on the nest and **incubating** the eggs. The male spends most of his time hunting for food for himself and for his mate. Once the eggs have hatched, the female stays near the nest and looks after the young while the male finds food for the chicks. At first the female has to tear up the food into small pieces, but soon the chicks can tear up the food for themselves. Once the chicks are about half-grown, the female begins to leave the nest for periods of time to hunt for food.

Bald eagles build their nests in trees close to water. They use the same nests every year, and the nests can become very large.

Sibling rivalry

Eagles usually lay two eggs. However, the chick that hatches first is usually bigger, and the younger chick cannot compete for food. The younger chick may die of starvation, or sometimes the older chick pushes it out of the nest. If food is short, the older chick may eat the younger one.

Laying a second egg may seem like a waste of a female eagle's energy, since the chick usually dies. However, the second egg acts as a sort of insurance policy in case the first egg does not hatch or there is something wrong with the older chick. If food is plentiful, both chicks may survive.

MANY MOUTHS TO FEED

Most birds of prey form pairs to mate and bring up chicks, but there are exceptions to this rule. **Harriers** live in loose groups of around 20 to 40 birds. Each male mates with two or three females. A male harrier can have up to five different mates, and he has to supply all of them with food while they are incubating eggs. Once the eggs hatch, he also helps feed the chicks. With so many mouths to feed, the male does not waste time. He passes on food in an incredible mid-air transfer, where the female turns upside down beneath the male and catches the food that he drops to her.

31

Courtship in Other Birds

Birds rely heavily on their eyesight, so when they choose the best partner for mating, the courtship often involves visual displays. These may be courtship flights, like those of eagles and other birds of prey, or they may be courtship displays, where the males show off in some way to the female birds. In some species pairs do detailed courtship dances together.

Peacocks are capable of reproducing by the age of two, but their tail feathers are not fully developed. This means that they cannot compete with the displays of older peacocks with fully developed tails.

Amazing displays

In many different bird species, the plumage of male birds is adapted for display to females. Some birds have only a crest or a ruff of feathers, or colored patches on their plumage. In other birds the males have amazing colors and display feathers. Some species keep their breeding plumage all year, while others molt in the winter to a much duller plumage.

Some of the most amazing displays are found among birds from the mountains and forests of south and east Asia. In India, peacocks display their incredible tails. In China and Southeast Asia, colorful relatives such as the argus pheasant and the tragopan have displays that are equally impressive. Another group of birds with incredible plumage are the birds of paradise from the forests of New Guinea.

Outside of South and East Asia, there are plenty of other birds with impressive displays. Ground birds, such as grouse and bustards, fluff out and spread their feathers to make a fantastic courtship display. The greater painted snipe has a handsome courtship display, but in this case it is the female that displays to the male.

In all these birds, except the painted snipe, the males display and mate with as many females as they can attract. After mating, the males have little or nothing to do with incubation or raising chicks.

Couple dances

In some bird species, both males and females are involved in complex courtship dances. Japanese cranes begin their courtship dance when the male leaps high, with wings outstretched, inviting the female to join him. The pair then bow and strut around each other with their wings partly open. They may also run and take short flights as part of the ritual.

Divers and grebes do their courtship dances in the water. In grebes, the courtship may involve running on the water side by side, head bobbing and shaking, **preening**, and standing up out of the water breast to breast, with a beak full of waterweed.

In species that do paired courtship dances, the birds pair up for a season or, in the case of Japanese cranes, for life. Both males and females are involved in the incubation and care of the young.

This bower was constructed by a male bower bird. Bower birds collect all kinds of bright and colorful objects to decorate their bowers with.

DECORATED DISPLAYS

Bower birds are artists of the bird world. Instead of displaying their feathers, male bowerbirds build a spectacular bower (a thatched hut) out of sticks and grass. Then they decorate them with all kinds of objects.

Birdsong

Song is another important part of courtship for most birds. A song is a repeated pattern of notes that is usually sung by male birds in the breeding season to defend their territory, or to attract the attention of females.

Birds make other calls besides singing during the breeding season. This fledgling yellow-headed blackbird may be making an alarm call.

From booms to trills

There is an incredible variety of bird songs, from the loud booming calls of the bittern to the trilling and warbling songs of birds such as warblers. Nearly all this singing is done by male birds.

Males sing for two reasons. First, each male stakes out his territory using singing. The male's territorial song is short, but loud and far-reaching. It tells other males that this male is strong and able to defend his territory.

The second reason that male birds sing is to attract female birds. A male's courtship song is longer and more complicated than his territorial song. The male tries to impress female birds with the strength and variety of his songs. Only a healthy and strong bird can sing loudly and continuously for days on end.

Getting the message across

In a rich habitat, such as a forest, many different birds sing at the same time. The result could be an awful noise, but in fact this is not the case. Different birds' songs are adapted to fit in with the songs of other birds in the habitat. This is important because a bird whose message is drowned out by the songs of other birds will not be able to attract the attention of females, and so will not mate.

Males usually sing from a high perch, because their song travels farther from a height. In the grassland habitats where larks live, however, there are no places to perch. Larks make a special singing flight in which they sing as they spiral higher and higher into the sky.

A DOUBLE VOICE BOX

The human larynx (voice box) is near the top of the windpipe. It has two flaps of muscle with a thin slit between them. As air passes through the slit, the flaps of muscle vibrate and produce sounds.

A bird's **syrinx**, on the other hand, is at the bottom of the windpipe where it splits into two. There are slits in each of the two airways, so a bird basically has two voice boxes. This is part of the reason why birds can sing so well.

New Zealand kakapos make even louder calls than bitterns. Kakapos amplify their booming calls by clearing a shallow bowl of earth and using it as a sort of amplifier. The call can be heard from over 4.5 miles (7 kilometers) away.

Nesting and Young

A bird's nest is an adaptation to help protect the eggs and, once they hatch, the young birds. A nest is often a cup-shaped structure built in a tree. The nest hides the eggs from predators, stops them from rolling away, and keeps the eggs close together to make them easy to incubate. There are many other kinds of nests, however, from shallow holes in the ground to large group nests that spread across a whole group of trees.

Eagle nests

Eagles and other birds of prey usually nest in the same places year after year. There are often several nest sites in an eagle's territory, and each year the eagles repair one of the nests. One bald eagle nest that had been used for many years weighed 1 ton (1,000 kilos). Many eagles nest in large, open-crowned trees, but golden eagles prefer nesting sites on cliffs.

Birds build a wide variety of nests, such as (a) a woodpecker's hole nest, (b) the woven nest of a weaver bird, (c) two overbird mud nests, and (d) an eagle's platform nest.

Other birds

Nests are often made from grasses, twigs, and other plant material, and are lined with soft materials such as wool. Many swallows and swifts build flask-shaped or bowl-shaped nests out of mud. A relative of swifts, the cave swiftlet builds its tiny hammock-shaped nest from **saliva**. The nests of these birds are the main ingredient of bird's nest soup, a traditional Chinese food.

Many ground-nesting birds make a shallow hole in the ground for a nest. Most of these birds have camouflaged eggs, like those of plovers (see page 21). Birds such as kingfishers, woodpeckers, and storm petrels dig their own burrows to nest in. Other birds—such as hornbills, pigeons, and falcons—lay their eggs in holes that they find in trees or cliffs.

Hatching time

Birds incubate their eggs for between 12 and 60 days. At the end of this time, the chicks hatch out. In over half of all birds—including wrens, finches, and thrushes—the chicks are blind and featherless when they hatch. The adult birds feed their chicks for several weeks before they are strong enough to leave the nest and begin to fly.

Other birds—such as ducks, swifts, hummingbirds—and ground-nesting birds, such as chickens and grouse, hatch with **down** and open eyes. They are active soon after hatching and begin to feed themselves within a few hours or days.

MASTER BUILDERS

Weaver birds are probably the most expert of all nest builders. There are many different species, but they all make nests by weaving together grasses or other strands of plant material. The most common species, the southern masked weaver, builds flask-shaped nests that hang from the branches of trees. Social weavers work together to make a large roof over a nesting colony of up to 300 nests.

Kingfishers usually nest in a hole on a riverbank. The chicks are born blind and helpless. They take three to four weeks to fledge (learn to fly).

Eagles on the Edge

Eagles are top predators, so they have no natural enemies. However, humans and their activities have proved to be worse enemies than any predator.

Many eagles will face extinction if humans continue to destroy their habitats.

A bad reputation

For hundreds of years, people hunted and killed eagles. There are stories of eagles carrying off babies, and farmers blamed eagles for killing their lambs. This constant hunting greatly reduced the populations of many eagle species. White-tailed sea eagles were wiped out in the United Kingdom, and golden eagles disappeared from all of the United Kingdom except Scotland.

Thinly spread

Eagle populations are thinly spread in most places where they live. For every eagle there has to be many prey animals for the eagle to eat, and even more plants for the prey animals to feed on. This means that a habitat can support fewer eagles than it can other animals.

When a habitat is damaged or destroyed—for instance, when forest is cut down to make space for farmland—birds of prey are the first to suffer. They need larger areas of habitat than other animals to keep them alive, so they cannot survive if their habitat is broken up into small pieces. A pair of martial eagles, for example, needs an area of between 48 and 116 square miles (125 and 300 square kilometers) to survive and bring up chicks.

Eagles are also badly affected by some types of **pollutants** in the environment, which get concentrated higher up the **food chain**. After **pesticides** (chemicals for killing insects) are sprayed onto crops, plant-eaters have more of the pollutant in them than plants. Meat-eaters, in turn, have higher concentrations of pollutant than plant-eaters.

Eagles endangered

Some eagles have not been able to adapt to the many threats to their survival. About a quarter of all birds of prey are in danger of extinction, including several eagles. The great Philippine eagle is one of the most endangered animals in the world. The Madagascar fish eagle is found only along a 373-mile (600-kilometer) stretch of coast in Madagascar.

A CLOSE SHAVE

In the 1960s, bald eagles came very close to becoming **extinct**. In the 1950s and 1960s, it was found that a pesticide called DDT was damaging bald eagle eggs. The shells of the eggs were so thin that they broke when their parents incubated them. As a result, few bald eagles managed to raise chicks, and they became very rare. The use of DDT was banned in the United States in 1972, and eagle populations have begun to recover.

White-tailed eagles were reintroduced into northern Scotland between 1975 and 1985. A small breeding population of the birds is now slowly growing. Banners encourage members of the public to report any suspicious activity that may endanger the eagles.

OPERATION EASTER MULL EAGLE WATCH

If you see anything suspicious contact:
Oban Police Office   Tel: 01631 562213
Salen Police Office   Tel: 01680 ___

Forest Enterprise   STRATHCLYDE POLICE   RSPB

Winners and Losers

Birds of prey are not the only birds to be affected by human activities. More than 500 kinds of birds around the world are in danger of becoming extinct because of changes humans have made to the environment. A small number of birds have, however, adapted successfully to living around humans.

Declining numbers

Destruction of habitat is the main cause of falling bird numbers. The worst effects are in tropical rainforests, which are home to nearly half of all bird species. Large areas of rainforest have been cut down for timber and to make way for roads and farms. As a result, some rainforest birds are now extinct, and many more are in danger of dying out.

Island birds are especially in danger of extinction because there were only small populations of them in the first place. One cause of the destruction of island birds is the introduction of animals such as rats and cats that are not native to the island. The island birds have no defenses against these animals. In New Zealand, cats and rats have killed huge numbers of flightless birds that are found nowhere else in the world. The kakapo, a large flightless parrot, is now extinct in the wild, although some birds live on small protected islands where there are no predators.

The hyacinth macaw is the largest and one of the rarest macaws. It is now considered to be an endangered species.

Adapting to humans

A few birds have adapted to life among humans and have done very well. Black kites are **scavengers** that have adapted to living on the garbage dumps of cities throughout North Africa, the Middle East, and South Asia. Birds such as sparrows, starlings, and blackbirds also have adapted to living in cities. Most of these birds are generalists.

However, at least one specialist that has adapted to human habitats is the little ringed plover. These birds originally lived on mud flats along coasts and on short grasslands. Today, they have adapted to breeding in gravel pits, on garbage dumps, and in many other industrial areas.

Some birds of prey have also adapted to living close to humans. Kestrels are now probably the most numerous birds of prey in the world. Peregrine falcons naturally live on cliffs, and in many large cities they have adapted to living on tall buildings.

Peregrine falcons have adapted to living in cities, building their nests high up on tall buildings.

DISAPPEARING SPARROWS

House sparrows have lived close to humans for hundreds of years. However, over the past 30 years, scientists have noticed large drops in sparrow populations in some places. In eastern England, for instance, numbers have fallen by 90 percent since the 1970s. The large numbers of pet cats may be responsible for this decline, or it may be due to a chemical added to lead-free gasoline. Another possibility for the house sparrow's decline is the radiation from mobile phones. Nobody really knows for sure why numbers have declined, although many scientists are doing research to try to find out.

Bird History

In 1861 a **fossilized** creature was found in a slate quarry in Germany. The animal was about 150 million years old. It was so well preserved that the feathers covering its body could still be seen. The fossil was named archaeopteryx. Although many other bird fossils have been found since 1861, archaeopteryx is still the best example of a bird ancestor.

A selection of extinct birds includes the following:
(a) archaeopteryx,
(b) teratornid, (c) giant moa,
and (d) elephant bird.

Tiny dinosaurs

Archaeopteryx had feathers like a bird, but it also had a long tail like a lizard. It had a beak, but it also had teeth. It had feathers and wings, but it still had claws on its front limbs.

Studies of archaeopteryx and many other fossils have led scientists to think that birds are descended from one group of dinosaurs known as theropods. This is the group of dinosaurs that tyrannosaurus belonged to, although tyrannosaurus became extinct long before birds evolved. It is now known that some theropods had feathers.

Giant birds

Some fossils of birds from the past are much bigger than modern birds. For instance, diatryma was a flightless bird standing 7 feet 3 inches (2.2 meters) tall. It is thought to have been a fierce predator. Diatryma lived 55 to 65 million years ago, but more recently there were even bigger birds. In New Zealand, moas grew to a height of 11 feet 6 inches (3.5 meters). These are the tallest birds ever known. In Madagascar another giant bird, the elephant bird, was the heaviest bird ever known. It weighed up to 1,100 pounds (500 kilograms). It is not known how diatryma became extinct, but both the moas and the elephant birds were hunted to extinction in historical times.

Passenger pigeons were hunted to extinction in the 20th century.

PASSENGER PIGEONS

In the 18th century, there were 3 billion passenger pigeons in North America. These pigeons lived in huge groups of millions of birds. Passenger pigeons were good to eat and so they were hunted for food, even when they began to get scarce. By 1900 there were no passenger pigeons in the wild, and the last one in a zoo died in 1914. This example shows how even common species can be wiped out in just a short time.

Failing to adapt

Another group of giant birds became extinct for other reasons. Teratornids were giant, vulture-like birds that lived until about 10,000 years ago. The largest known teratornid, a fossil of which was found recently in Argentina, had a wingspan of over 23 feet (7 meters)!

Teratornids probably fed on the carcasses of large animals, such as sabertooth cats and mammoths. However, about 10,000 years ago, many large mammals suddenly died out. Then teratornids also died out, probably because their main food source died out and they were unable to adapt to the change.

Today, many modern birds are failing to adapt to changes caused by humans. Humans need to adapt to live alongside birds and other animals, rather than hunting them and destroying their habitats. If people can do this, the rich variety of bird life on Earth will survive.

Further Information

Classification of birds of prey

Birds of prey are divided into two large groups known as orders—the daytime birds of prey (Falconiformes) and the owls (Strigiformes). Within the two orders, the birds are divided further into families:

Order Falconiformes

Family	Number of species	Examples
New World vultures	7	condors and vultures found in North and South America
secretary bird	1	The secretary bird is the only remaining species of this family. Fossils of two other species are known.
osprey	1	another family with only one species
		falcons, kestrels, and sparrow hawks
eagles, hawks, and buzzards	234	eagles, hawks, buzzards, and Old World vultures (vultures from Africa, Asia, and Europe)

Order Strigiformes

Family	Number of species	Examples
typical owls	189	tawny owls, screech owls, eagle owls, snowy owls, and many others
barn owls	17	barn owls, grass owls, and bay owls

Record-breaking birds

Biggest	ostrich	9 ft. (2.75 m) tall, weight 345 lb. (156 kg)
Smallest	bee hummingbird	2.5 in. (6.2 cm) long, weight only 0.06 oz. (1.6 g)
Fastest flying (diving)	peregrine falcon	124 mph (200 km/h)
Fastest level flight	wandering albatross	35 mph (56 km/h)
Fastest runner	ostrich	males can easily run at 45 mph (72 km/h)
Longest migratory flight	arctic tern	they breed on the shores of the Arctic Ocean, then fly to the Antarctic
Highest recorded flight	Ruppell's griffon vulture	37,000 ft. (11,277 m). At this height human beings would die from a lack of oxygen.
Keenest vision	peregrine falcon	can see a pigeon at a distance of 5 mi. (8 km)
Keenest hearing	barn owl and relatives	can catch a rodent in complete darkness
Biggest bill	Australian pelican	up to 18.5 in. (47 cm)
Most feathers	tundra swan	25,216 feathers

Books

- Newton, Ian. *Birds of Prey*. New York: Weldon Owen, 2000.
  – Illustrated guide to the 292 species of raptors

- Solway, Andrew. *Wild Predators: Birds of Prey*. Chicago: Heinemann Library, 2005.
  – Book that explores the lives of a variety of exciting birds of prey

Websites

- Birds of Prey Foundation
  www.birds-of-prey.org
  – Organization that cares for injured and orphaned birds

- National Audubon Society
  www.audubon.org
  – The most important bird conservation society in the United States

- The Peregrine Fund: The World Center for Birds of Prey
  www.peregrinefund.org
  – International bird conservation society

Glossary

accipiter eagle, hawk, buzzard, or other daytime bird of prey that builds a nest

adaptation change that helps a living thing fit into its environment

algae tiny plant-like living things. Seaweed is an example of algae.

bill bird's beak

camouflage coloring and patterning that help an animal hide from its enemies or blend into its environment

carcass dead body of an animal

carrion dead and rotting meat

cell tiny building block of all living things

diet range of foods an animal eats

down soft fine feathers of a bird that provide insulation

echolocation location of objects by reflected sounds

evolution process by which life on Earth has developed and changed

extinct when all animals of a certain species die out

fledge when young birds first learn to fly

food chain series of plants and animals, each of which is food for the next

fossilized hardened and turned to rock in the ground

gamete male or female sex cell, usually sperm or egg

gene something that is transferred from a parent to its offspring that determines some features of that offspring

generalist living thing that can live in a variety of habitats

habitat place where an animal lives

harrier small hawk with excellent hearing that hunts in reeds and other habitats where prey is hard to see

home range area around a bird's nesting site where it hunts for food

incubate keep eggs warm so that they will hatch

mate animal's breeding partner; also, when a male and female animal come together to produce young

migrate travel long distances each year from a summer breeding area to a winter feeding ground

mob dive at and harass a larger bird as a group

molt when a bird gradually loses its old feathers, which are replaced with new feathers

natural selection mechanism of evolution by which only those individuals that are best fitted to their habitat and lifestyle survive and reproduce

nectar sugary fluid in flowers

offspring young of an animal

omnivore animal that eats both plant and animal food

parasite living thing that lives and feeds on or inside another living thing

pesticide chemical that is used to kill insects, spiders, or other small creatures that feed on farm crops

plumage bird's coat of feathers

pollutant something that causes damage to the environment

predator animal that hunts and kills other animals for food

preening cleaning and arranging the feathers

prey animal that is eaten by a predator

primate group of mammals that includes monkeys, apes, and humans

range places where a living thing is known to live

regurgitate bring swallowed food back up to the mouth

reproduce produce young

roost place where birds sleep or rest

saliva watery liquid in the mouth

savannah area of mixed grassland and thorny trees

scavenger animal that feeds on dead and rotting animals or other kinds of waste

specialist living thing that is adapted to a particular habitat

species group of very similar animals that can breed together to produce healthy offspring

streamline smooth the shape of something so that it slips easily through air or water

syrinx bird's voice box

talon hooked claw

territory area around a bird's nest, usually smaller than the home range, that birds defend against other birds of the same species

thermal area of warm, rising air

top predator predator at the top of the food chain that is not the prey of another animal

variation difference among individuals within a species

vertebrate animal with a backbone, such as mammals, birds, reptiles, and amphibians

warm-blooded able to keep the body at a constant temperature

Index